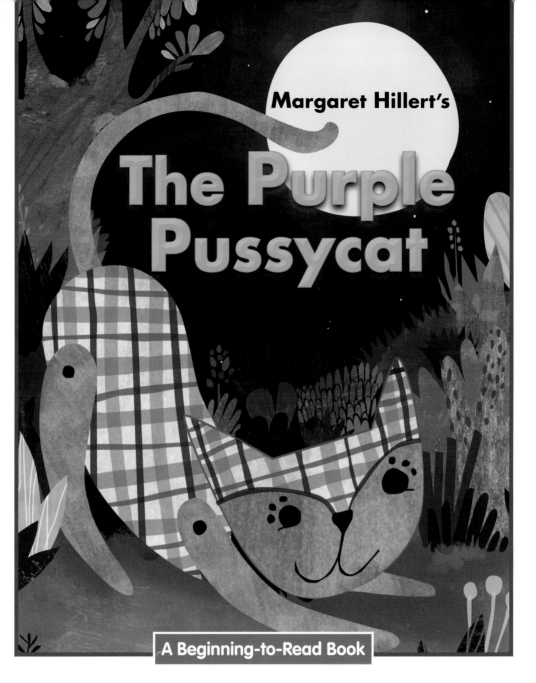

Margaret Hillert's

The Purple Pussycat

A Beginning-to-Read Book

Illustrated by Kate Cosgrove

DEAR CAREGIVER,

The books in this Beginning-to-Read collection may look somewhat familiar in that the original versions could have been a part of your own early reading experiences. These carefully written texts feature common sight words to provide your child multiple exposures to the words appearing most frequently in written text. These new versions have been updated and the engaging illustrations are highly appealing to a contemporary audience of young readers.

Begin by reading the story to your child, followed by letting him or her read familiar words and soon your child will be able to read the story independently. At each step of the way, be sure to praise your reader's efforts to build his or her confidence as an independent reader. Discuss the pictures and encourage your child to make connections between the story and his or her own life. At the end of the story, you will find reading activities and a word list that will help your child practice and strengthen beginning reading skills. These activities, along with the comprehension questions are aligned to current standards, so reading efforts at home will directly support the instructional goals in the classroom.

Above all, the most important part of the reading experience is to have fun and enjoy it!

Shannon Cannon

Shannon Cannon,
Literacy Consultant

Norwood House Press • www.norwoodhousepress.com
Beginning-to-Read™ is a registered trademark of Norwood House Press. All Rights Reserved.
Illustration and cover design copyright ©2017 by Norwood House Press. All Rights Reserved.

Authorized adapted reprint from the U.S. English language edition, entitled The Purple Pussycat by Margaret Hillert. Copyright © 2017 Margaret Hillert. Reprinted with permission. All rights reserved. Pearson and The Purple Pussycat are trademarks, in the US and/or other countries, of Pearson Education, Inc. or its affiliates. This publication is protected by copyright, and prior permission to re-use in any way in any format is required by both Norwood House Press and Pearson Education. This book is authorized in the United States for use in schools and public libraries.

Designer: Lindaanne Donohoe
Editorial Production: Lisa Walsh

LIBRARY OF CONGRESS CATALOGING-IN-PUBLICATION DATA
Names: Hillert, Margaret, author. I Cosgrove, Kate, illustrator.
Title: Purple pussycat / by Margaret Hillert ; illustrated by Kate Cosgrove.
Description: Chicago, IL : Norwood House Press, [2016] I Series: A Beginning-to-Read book I Originally published in 2007 by Norwood House Press. I Summary: "A stuffed pussycat comes to life at night and sets out to explore seeing what animals do during the night"– Provided by publisher.
Identifiers: LCCN 2016001869 (print) I LCCN 2016022197 (ebook) I ISBN 9781599538037 (library edition : alk. paper) I ISBN 9781603579650 (eBook)
Subjects: I CYAC: Toys–Fiction. I Animals–Fiction.
Classification: LCC PZ7.H558 Pu 2016 (print) I LCC PZ7.H558 (ebook) I DDC [E]–dc23
LC record available at https://lccn.loc.gov/2016001869

288N—072016
Manufactured in the United States of America in North Mankato, Minnesota.

We can not play now.
We have work to do.
Can you help me?

3

Now we can go.
Come with me.
I want you to come.

Here we are.
I like you here with me.
This is good.

I want to go out.
I will jump down.
Here I go.

You can play here.
You can have fun.
But I will go away.
You can not come with me.

Out, out I go.
Out to see what I can see.
This is fun.

Oh, look up.
Look up, up, up.
How big it is!
It is pretty.
I like it.

And see what is here.
Look at this.
One, two, three little ones.

The little ones jump.
The little ones run.
The little ones play.

13

I can run and jump, too.
I can play.
I like it out here.

Oh, oh.
What is this?
It looks like me.
It runs and jumps, too.
I can make it run.
What fun!

Something is up here.
What is it?
What is it?

Oh, I see you now.
You are big.
Who are you?
Who? Who?

And here is something little.
I see you, too.
You will have to run.

Run away, little one.
Run, run, run.
Something will get you.

Now I will go here.
What will I find here?
What will I see now?

I see you work.
I see what you have.
You will eat it.

Away I go.
Away I go
to see what I can see.

Oh, my.
Look at this.
What a good mother this is.

Here I am.
And in I go.
In, in, in.

You are here with me,
but we can get up now.
Get up. Get up.
Come out and play with me.

Foundational Skills

In addition to reading the numerous high-frequency words in the text, this book also supports the development of foundational skills.

Phonological Awareness: The /p/ sound

Oddity Task: Say the /**p**/ sound for your child. Ask your child to say the word that doesn't have the /**p**/ sound in the following word groups:

pat, tap, mat	park, mark, pack	set, pet, step	peach, reach, pea
met, pet, up	spot, top, ten	seat, sleep, keep	mark, spark, speck

Phonics: The letter Pp

1. Demonstrate how to form the letters **P** and **p** for your child.
2. Have your child practice writing **P** and **p** at least three times each.
3. Ask your child to point to the words in the book that have the letter **p** in them.
4. Write down the following words and ask your child to circle the letter **p** in each word:

play	help	pretty	puppy
jump	pop	skip	nap
peep	pan	pepper	stamp

Fluency: Choral Reading

1. Reread the story with your child at least two more times while your child tracks the print by running a finger under the words as they are read. Ask your child to read the words he or she knows with you.
2. Reread the story aloud together. Be careful to read at a rate that your child can keep up with.
3. Repeat choral reading and allow your child to be the lead reader and ask him or her to change from a whisper to a loud voice while you follow along and change your voice.

Language

The concepts, illustrations, and text in this book help children develop language both explicitly and implicitly.

Vocabulary: Opposites

1. The story features the concepts of big and little. Discuss opposites and ask your child to name the opposites of the following:

in (out)	up (down)	play (work)	good (bad)	hard (soft)
happy (sad)	tall (short)	clean (dirty)	quiet (loud)	old (new)

2. Write each of the words on separate pieces of paper. Mix the words up and ask your child to put the opposite pairs back together.

Reading Literature and Informational Text

To support comprehension, ask your child the following questions. The answers either come directly from the text or require inferences and discussion.

Key Ideas and Detail

- Ask your child to retell the sequence of events in the story.
- Why does the Purple Pussycat tell the mouse to run away on page 23?

Craft and Structure

- Is this a book that tells a story or one that gives information? How do you know?
- Do you think the purple pussycat wanted to get up and play in the morning?

Integration of Knowledge and Ideas

- What are the little animals that jump, run and play in the story?
- Can you tell a story about an adventure your favorite stuffed animal might have when you're asleep?

WORD LIST

The Purple Pussycat uses the 59 words listed below.

This list can be used to practice reading the words that appear in the text. You may wish to write the words on index cards and use them to help your child build automatic word recognition. Regular practice with these words will enhance your child's fluency in reading connected text.

a	get	make	the
am	go	me	this
and	good	Mother	three
are		my	to
at	have		too
away	help	not	two
	here	now	
big	how		up
but		oh	
	I	one(s)	want
can	in	out	we
come	is		what
	it	play	who
do		pretty	will
down	jump(s)		with
		run(s)	work
eat	like		
	little	see	you
find	look(s)	something	
fun			

ABOUT THE AUTHOR Margaret Hillert has helped millions of children all over the world learn to read independently. She was a first grade teacher for 34 years and during that time started writing books that her students could both gain confidence in reading and enjoy. She wrote well over 100 books for children just learning to read. As a child, she enjoyed writing poetry and continued her poetic writings as an adult for both children and adults.

Photograph by Glenna Washburn

ABOUT THE ILLUSTRATOR Kate Cosgrove is a professional artist and illustrator. She lives in Michigan with her husband, daughter, elderly dog and grumpy three-legged cat. www.katecosgrove.com